TENREC'S TWIGS

BERT KITCHEN

Philomel Books

NEW YORK

As the sun rose over the hill, Tenrec popped his head out of his burrow and sniffed the fresh morning air.

The weather was dry and bright, just right for building. He snuffled along until he came to the place where he had gathered a pile of twigs the day before.

He walked around the twigs several times, humming happily. Then he began to build.

He pushed thick twigs into the ground in a circle, and rested more twigs on these. Then he chose twigs that seemed springy and bendy, and wove them in and out, stepping back from time to time to see how the shape was coming along.

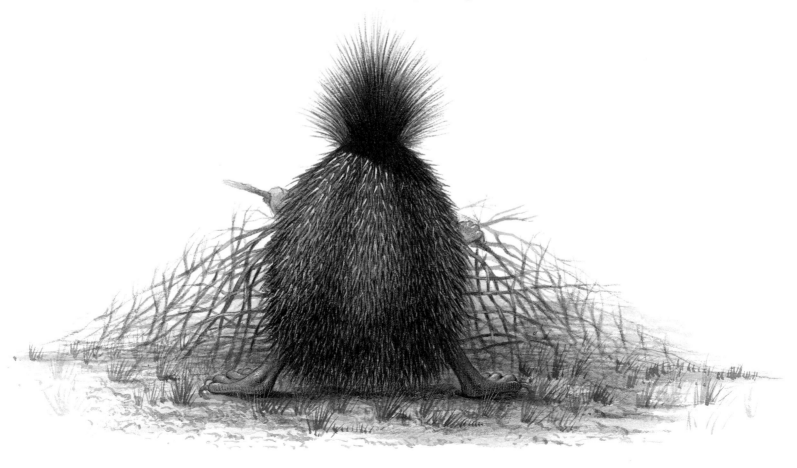

Then Old Warthog came by. He could be grumpy at the best of times, but today he was feeling particularly miserable. He plonked his hoof right on the side of Tenrec's twig building.

"Useless! A waste of time!" he grumbled. "Ask any of the other animals."

And he went on his way.

Tenrec was upset. Useless, he thought. A waste of time? He decided he would ask some of the other animals.

Tenrec spied Grey Parrot on a branch above him. Before he could even ask the question, Grey Parrot squawked, "Useless! Useless! A waste of time."

"I haven't even asked you the question," Tenrec said. Then he realized that Grey Parrot had overheard Old Warthog. He was simply repeating what he had heard.

"I'll ask someone else," Tenrec said to himself. Soon he came across Giant Anteater. He asked him what he thought of his twigs.

   "Strange as it seems," said Anteater, "although I do have a long nose, I don't really like poking it into other creatures' business. So I wouldn't like to say. But I have just seen Pangolin hanging about. Why not ask him?"

Tenrec found Pangolin hanging by his tail from a high branch. To get closer Tenrec quickly made a small twig platform and asked him his question.

But Pangolin was so wrapped up in himself and his own thoughts, he could not even be bothered to try to understand. "Twigs? Buildings, Tenrec?" he said in an absent-minded voice.

Tenrec was feeling no happier. Then he spotted Giraffe munching leaves way up in the trees above him. It seemed as though Giraffe's head were in the clouds. Tenrec tapped him on the hoof to get his attention.

"Giraffe, I don't know if you have noticed my little twig buildings," Tenrec asked politely, "but do you think I should stop building them?"

Giraffe bent down, "I've never noticed your twigs, Tenrec, so I have no feeling for or against them." With that he straightened up and his head disappeared into the leaves again.

J ust then Tenrec saw Golden Mole shuffling along, looking for food. Surely he will see things my way, thought Tenrec. So he said to Mole, "Do you think I am foolish to make my twig buildings?"

"I spend most of my time underground in the dark, Tenrec. I can see little or nothing out here. I am afraid I know nothing about your buildings."

Just as Mole finished speaking, Adjutant Stork came strutting along. Tenrec put his question to the tall bird.

Adjutant Stork puffed out his chest, looking very important. "Well," he said, "in my opinion . . . as a matter of fact . . . perhaps . . ." but, overcome by his own importance, he completely forgot the question and began to strut away.

Tenrec was beginning to lose heart when he came upon Two-Toed Sloth hanging sleepily from the bough of a tree. "Sloth," he said, "Do you think I should stop building my twigs? Warthog says there is no use for them."

Now Sloth was extremely slow. Finally he said, "Ask me again tomorrow, Tenrec, or better still next week (yawn) . . . It is such a difficult question (yawn) that I need plenty of time (yawn) in order to . . ." Before Sloth could finish the sentence he had fallen asleep.

Who else could Tenrec ask? Did nobody care about his twigs? Then Tenrec remembered Milky Eagle Owl. He made his way to Owl's perching place where he knew the bird spent many hours just sitting and thinking.

"Please, Owl," he asked, "do you think my twig-building is useless and a waste of time?"

Owl closed his eyes for several seconds, then said, "Hmmm, I find your twig building very interesting, Tenrec. You seem very happy when you are building and you certainly do not bother me, hmmm, or anyone else. In fact you may inspire others to build. My advice is to continue building!"

ow Tenrec had his answer. Humming happily, he went
back to his building and pushed another twig into
the ground.

Animals In The Story

in order of appearance

All the animals in this story exist, even though they may look too weird and wonderful to be true. Most of them come from central and southern Africa.

The main character in this story is a **Streaked Tenrec.** Tenrecs are small creatures, resembling something between a shrew and a hedgehog and are found only on the island of Madagascar. Tenrecs are inquisitive, tenacious little animals, and are very active. Their habitat is being destroyed, but they have not yet been declared a protected species as some of the larger animals from that part of the world have been. Without protection they may soon become extinct.

Warthogs get their name from the two large warts or protuberances they have on each side of their heads. The old, darker boars are usually loners.

The **African Grey Parrot** is renowned for its outstanding ability to mimic the human voice. Parrots are known to live up to 50 years, sometimes even longer.

The **Giant Anteater,** as its name suggests, feeds on ants and termites. With its four strong claws on its forelegs the anteater rips open the muddy walls of nests. It then inserts its long tongue, which is covered in sticky saliva so that the insects stick to it.

The **Small-scaled Pangolin** in this story is one of several types of pangolin. Using their long tails pangolins will spend much of their time climbing trees. They too have long and sticky tongues to help them catch their food.

The **Giraffe** is one of the tallest animals and feeds on leaves and fruit from the top of acacia and thorn trees. When drinking, the giraffe has to splay its front legs in order to stoop down.

The **Golden Mole** spends much of its time underground, and its eyes are almost lost now, being covered with hairy skin. Golden Moles have a sense of touch which they use looking for food, and a strong sense of smell which they use for finding new burrows, foraging for food and seeking partners for breeding.

The **Marabou "Adjutant" Stork** acquired its name because of its pompous measured walk which reminded British colonial troops of adjutant officers. Although ungainly when on the ground adjutant storks fly well and can soar like vultures.

The **Two-toed Sloth** is very inactive and sluggish in its movements. Sloths spend much of their time hanging face upwards, from the branches of trees, suspended by their hooked claws.

The **Milky Eagle Owl** like many other owls, hunts at twilight. By day these owls perch on rocks or trees camouflaged by their plumage. They sit with eyes almost closed, but the slightest noise arouses them. The owl has been associated with wisdom since ancient times.

For Thomas, Katie and David

Text and illustrations copyright © 1989 by Bert Kitchen.
Published by Philomel Books, a division of The Putnam & Grosset Group,
200 Madison Avenue, New York, NY 10016. All rights reserved.
Published simultaneously in Great Britain by Lutterworth Press/James Clarke & Co. Ltd.
Published simultaneously in Canada. First American edition 1989.
Printed in England by Purnell Book Production Limited

Library of Congress Catologing-in-Publication Data

Kitchen, Bert. Tenrec's twigs.   Summary: Seized with doubts about the value of the
small buildings he constructs out of twigs, Tenrec goes from one jungle animal to the
next asking for opinions.   [1. Tenrecs–Fiction. 2. Jungle animals–Fiction]
I. Title   PZ7.K67124Te   1989   [E]   88-25389   ISBN 0-399-21720-7
First Impression